We followed the man.

He walked slowly. He looked at all the people who walked by.

"He's in a shopping mall," Houdini whispered, "but he isn't shopping. That's suspicious."

The man looked at his watch.

Suddenly, he turned and started walking fast. He headed straight toward a woman with a large shopping bag.

He reached out his hand.

"This is it," I said. "He's about to steal again. And this time we're going to catch him!"

The Houdini Club Magic Mystery series
by David A. Adler

A Houdini Club Magic Mystery

Magic Money

by David A. Adler

illustrated by Heather Harms Maione

A FIRST STEPPING STONE BOOK

Random House New York

For my nephew, Hillel,
and to his lovely bride, Tamar

Text copyright © 1997 by David A. Adler
Illustrations copyright © 1997 by Heather Harms Maione
"The Magic Money Trick" copyright © 1997 by Bob Friedhoffer
All rights reserved under International and Pan-American Copyright
Conventions. Published in the United States by Random House, Inc., New York,
and simultaneously in Canada by Random House of Canada Limited, Toronto.

http://www.randomhouse.com/

Library of Congress Cataloging-in-Publication Data
Adler, David A. Magic money / by David A. Adler ;
illustrated by Heather Harms Maione.
p. cm. — (A Houdini Club magic mystery) "A First stepping stone book."
SUMMARY: Herman "Houdini" Foster and his cousin Janet investigate an apparent
theft at the local mall.
ISBN 0-679-84699-9 (trade) — ISBN 0-679-94699-3 (lib. bdg.)
[1. Cousins—Fiction. 2. Shopping malls—Fiction. 3. Mystery and detective
stories.] I. Maione, Heather Harms, ill. II. Title. III. Series. PZ7.A2615Mag
1997 [Fic]—dc21 96-48205

Printed in the United States of America 10 9 8 7 6 5 4 3 2 1

A HOUDINI CLUB MAGIC MYSTERY is a trademark of Random House, Inc.

$ Contents $

1
Magic Money

"What you're doing is against the law," I told Houdini. "You could get arrested."

My cousin Houdini Foster was standing by the kitchen table. He was holding a green marker and a ruler. In front of him was a sheet of paper and a one-dollar bill. He was looking at the dollar bill and copying it.

"You can get into *real* trouble for making counterfeit money," I told him.

"I'm not making counterfeit money," Houdini said. He drew George Washington's nose. "I'm making Magic Money."

Houdini spread out his arms and said, "I, the Great Houdini, can tear this Magic Money in half and then make it whole again!"

Houdini bowed. Then he drew George Washington's hair.

So what! I thought. I could make a torn dollar whole again, too. I would use tape.

That's what I thought. But I didn't say it. If I did, Houdini probably would have shouted, "I, the Great Houdini, don't use tape!"

I was tired of hearing how great he is. To me, he's just my cousin.

His real name is Herman Foster.

Last year he read a book about Harry Houdini, who was once the world's greatest magician. After that my cousin practiced magic tricks. And he began calling *himself* Houdini. Now everyone calls him that.

I'm Janet Perry. And that's what everyone calls me.

Houdini's mother walked into the kitchen.

"Hello, Aunt Helen," I said.

"Hello, Janet. You look very pretty today."

She always says that, even when I look terrible. Aunt Helen is so nice.

Aunt Helen took some dishes out of the dishwasher and put them away. I helped her. I was putting a soup bowl in the cabinet when Houdini shouted, "ARE YOU READY FOR MAGIC?"

He shouted so loud, I almost dropped the bowl.

Houdini was wearing his black cape and top hat. He was standing on a kitchen chair. He had his Magic Money in one hand and an envelope in the other.

I put the bowl away and watched Houdini. Aunt Helen watched him, too. I think she was afraid he would fall off the chair.

"I will now call on someone from the audience to tear this dollar bill in half," Houdini said.

He gave the Magic Money to Aunt Helen.

"Tear it," he told her.

"Oh, no," she said. "It's a shame to tear this. It's so pretty."

I took the Magic Money from Aunt Helen and tore it. I like to tear things.

Houdini got off the chair. He put the torn Magic Money in the envelope. Then he licked the flap of the envelope and sealed it.

Houdini waved his hand over the envelope and said, "*Ala-kazam*, I am great. Yes, I am."

Those are his magic words.

Then Houdini tore off the end of the envelope and shook it. The Magic Money fell out.

Houdini smiled. It was one of his big magic show smiles. I could see his back teeth.

"I am great. Yes, I am," Houdini said again.

He held up the Magic Money. It was whole again! It wasn't torn. And it wasn't taped.

Houdini was right. It *was* Magic Money!

2
You Broke It,
You Bought It!

I looked real close at the Magic Money.
Houdini had drawn George Washington's
hair too long. He looked more like Martha.

Aunt Helen said, "That's amazing.
You're so smart."

Aunt Helen asked me, "Isn't he smart?"

"Yes," I said.

"I'm almost a genius," Houdini told us.

7

I looked at the Magic Money again. Houdini may be almost a genius, but he isn't a good artist. It was a terrible drawing of George Washington.

"That's a great trick. Will you teach me how you did it?" I asked.

Houdini took off his cape and hat. He put them in his backpack.

"I'll teach you at the club meeting."

Houdini was talking about the Houdini Club. He started it a few months ago. It's a magic club. There are nine of us in it. Once a week we meet in our friend Dana's basement. Each week Houdini shows us a new trick. After he does the trick, he teaches us how to do it.

Houdini looked at his watch.

"We have to hurry," he said to me,

"or we'll be late for the meeting."

I looked at my watch. It was noon. The meeting was at three o'clock.

"No, we won't. It's early," I said.

"Oh, no, it's not," Houdini said. Then he grabbed his backpack and rushed outside. I had to run to catch him.

"What's your hurry?" I asked. "The meeting isn't for another three hours. And anyway, you're always late."

We were already at the corner. Houdini stopped and asked, "Do you know what tomorrow is?"

"It's Sunday."

"It's Mother's Day," Houdini told me. "I have to go to the mall and buy my mom a gift."

"Oh, that," I said when we were across

the street. "I made my mom a card with felt and buttons. It's adorable. I made it two weeks ago.

"I made her a tile ashtray, too. My mom doesn't smoke. It's not good to smoke, you know. But she can use the ashtray for small things like hairpins. I'm keeping the card and ashtray at Dana's house so my mom won't find them."

"Good for you," Houdini said. But he didn't mean it. I think he was upset that I was ready for Mother's Day and he wasn't.

We didn't talk for a while. Then I said, "If we're going to the mall, I think you should know that last week a man had his wallet and shopping bag stolen. I read about it in the newspaper. It was lucky for him that he had his receipt in his pocket. The mall paid him for the stuff that was stolen from his shopping bag. But they didn't pay him for the stolen wallet."

"Don't worry about me," Houdini said.

We were at the entrance to the mall. Houdini looked at all the stores.

"Where should I go?"

I pointed to Fran's Fruit Fun and said, "Maybe you can buy your mother a fruit basket."

Houdini looked at me. He raised his right eyebrow. Then he raised his left eyebrow. He can do that. He's very talented.

"You're weird," Houdini said. "Fruit is something you eat because someone tells you to. It's not a gift."

Then Houdini pointed to a small store

in the corner of the mall, Sadie's Gift Shop. "That's where we'll go," Houdini said.

The store was filled with jewelry boxes, picture frames, and vases. Houdini picked

up a thin red vase. He turned it over to look at the price tag.

"Wow!" Houdini said. "This vase costs more than my bicycle."

"Be very careful. Don't break it," I

whispered. I pointed to a large sign.

YOU BROKE IT,
YOU BOUGHT IT!

Houdini very carefully put the vase back on the shelf.

He started walking to the door. "Let's get out of here," he whispered to me, "before I sneeze and break something."

When we were outside the store, I told Houdini, "Fruit baskets are not expensive. And they come in lots of sizes."

"I have a better idea," Houdini said. "I'll put a ribbon on some broccoli and give that to my mom."

Houdini was joking. Aunt Helen doesn't even like broccoli.

We looked through a few other stores in the mall. Houdini didn't find anything for Aunt Helen. Everything was too expensive.

Then we saw a sign in the window of Doug's Discounts.

MOTHER'S DAY GIFTS
$1 AND UP

"One dollar and up—that's for me," Houdini said. "Let's go to Doug's."

We had to cross the center of the mall to get to Doug's Discounts.

"Hey, watch out!" a woman shouted. She was pushing a carriage real fast and almost bumped into us.

We stopped. A man carrying a large shopping bag almost walked into us. He was looking all around, but not at where he was going.

"Excuse me," Houdini said real loud.

The man didn't even look at us. He just said, "Oh, yes," and kept walking.

Then, just as we came to the front of Doug's, we heard a woman shout.

"Help! Help! I've been robbed!"

3
I Was Robbed!

"There she is!" Houdini said.

Houdini ran over to the woman who screamed. I followed him. Other people ran over, too, including a security guard.

The woman was wearing a bright green dress. She was standing by one of the mall exits. On the floor next to her was a torn red shopping bag, a broken vase, and the wrapper from a Sugar Stick candy bar.

"He stole my wallet and all my money,"

the woman said. "Then he pulled at my shopping bag, but I wouldn't let go!"

"How terrible!" gasped someone in the crowd.

The guard took out a pad. He wrote down what the woman said.

"I just bought this beautiful vase, and he broke it."

The woman took a receipt from her pocket and showed it to the guard.

"I bought it at Sadie's Gift Shop a few minutes ago. See?"

The guard looked at the receipt. I stood on my tippy-toes and looked at it, too. It had the date and time printed on it. The time said 12:35 P.M.

I looked at my watch. It was 12:40 P.M.

"Look how much the vase cost," the

woman said. "It was very expensive."

The guard looked at the receipt again.

"Oh, my," he said. "It *was* expensive."

"Of course it was expensive," Houdini whispered to me. "It was from Sadie's."

The guard asked the woman to describe the thief.

"He was tall," the woman said. "But not so tall. He had brown hair with a little black in it, I think. And he looked angry. I remember that."

"What was he wearing?" the guard asked.

"I think he was wearing a coat. But I'm not sure. And did I tell you about his sneakers? He was wearing blue sneakers."

"Did you see which way he went?" the guard asked.

The woman pointed to the left, toward the center of the mall.

"We'll do everything we can to find the thief," the guard said. "Now, please come with me so you can fill out a report."

"Will I get repaid for the broken vase?" the woman asked.

"I'll talk to my boss," the guard said. "I think I can get you the money."

Houdini and I picked up the six large pieces from the broken vase. We gave them to the woman.

"What good are these?" she asked.

She left the broken vase and the torn bag there and walked off with the guard.

Houdini and I put the six pieces in the bag. We put the bag in the nearest trash basket.

I told Houdini, "I feel bad for that woman."

"Me too," Houdini said. "Now let's go back to Doug's. I have to buy a gift for my mom."

"But what about the thief?" I asked.

"What about him?"

"Aren't we going to look for him?"

"Later," Houdini told me. "My mom comes first."

We walked into Doug's. Right in front was a tower of tomato soup cans.

"Houdini," I said.

He looked at me and did his eyebrow thing. Then he told me, "I'm not giving my mom tomato soup for Mother's Day."

"That's not what I was going to say. I was going to ask you why the thief ran into the *center* of the mall and not out the exit."

"Maybe he wanted to get lost in the crowd," Houdini said. "Or maybe he wanted to rob someone else."

Rob someone else!

"Houdini, I really think we should look for him."

Houdini didn't answer me. He walked past the aisle with pencils and envelopes and pads of paper. Then he walked past the aisle with hand creams, mouthwash, and plastic bowls. There were goldfish and birds in the next aisle, and all the things you need to keep them as pets.

"I could get my mom a goldfish," Houdini said.

Then he said, "You're so cute."

He wasn't talking to me. He was talking to a fish.

I said, "Houdini, the thief may be robbing someone right now!"

Houdini sighed. "Life is never easy for an almost genius."

He waved good-bye to the goldfish.

"All right," he said. "Let's find that thief."

4
Blue Sneakers

We left the store. We walked to the center of the mall, where the woman said the thief ran.

"Look," I said. I pointed to a man. "He's tall and he has brown hair. He could be the thief."

Houdini looked at the man.

"He can't be the thief," Houdini said. "The woman said the thief *wasn't* so tall. And she said he had black in his hair."

Houdini pointed to someone else. "*He* could be the thief."

"But that man isn't wearing a coat," I told Houdini. "And I'm sure the woman said the thief was wearing a coat."

"No, she didn't. She said he *might* be wearing a coat. She wasn't sure."

"Well," I said. "How are we going to find the thief if we can't even agree what he looks like?"

"So let's agree," Houdini said. "You know I'm always right. And I say the thief is short, has black hair, and is not wearing a coat."

"This time you're wrong. The thief is tall, has brown hair, and *is* wearing a coat!" I said.

I folded my arms and looked at Houdini.

Houdini stared back at me. He gave me his "I'm right, you're wrong" look.

I thought for a minute. Then I said, "This is silly. The woman didn't give a very good description of the thief. We don't know how tall he is, or what color hair he has, or whether he's wearing a coat."

Houdini said, "But we do know the thief is a man. And we know he's wearing blue sneakers."

"*Red* sneakers," I said.

Houdini looked at me.

I smiled. "Just kidding."

We started looking for a man wearing blue sneakers. We walked through the mall with our heads down, looking at feet.

"I'm sorry," I said. I had bumped into an old woman.

"That's all right," she said. "You didn't hurt me."

"I'm sorry," Houdini said. He had bumped into a sign.

The sign didn't say, "That's all right."

We looked at hundreds of feet. None of them were in blue sneakers.

I told Houdini, "We'll never find the thief."

Houdini put his finger to his lips. He pointed to a man. The sneakers he was wearing were mostly white. But across the toes was a wide blue stripe.

$ 5 $
An Old Spy Trick

The man was tall. He had black hair and a bushy beard. He was wearing a coat.

We followed the man. He walked slowly. He looked at all the people who walked by.

"He's in a shopping mall," whispered Houdini, "but he isn't shopping. That's suspicious."

The man stopped in front of a shoe store. He looked in the window for a long time.

Houdini grabbed my hand and pulled me away.

"Why did you do that?" I asked.

"He's watching us," Houdini told me.

I turned and looked at the man. He was still looking in the shoe store window.

"He's not watching us," I said. "He's looking at shoes."

"It's an old spy trick," Houdini told me. He pulled me to a bench. "He's looking at our reflections in the window. I think he knows we're following him!"

We sat on the bench.

Houdini pretended to be talking to me.

"Inka, binka, tuna fish."

And I pretended to be talking to him.

"Tippy, sippy, chocolate soda."

We were really watching the man.

I asked Houdini, "How could the woman look at him and miss his beard?"

"Missing," Houdini mumbled. "Missing. Something is probably missing."

The man turned from the shoe store window and looked at the people walking by. Then he walked slowly to the bookstore.

Houdini wasn't watching the man with the beard anymore. Houdini was thinking.

The man looked in the bookstore window. Then he looked at his watch.

Suddenly he turned and started walking fast. He headed straight toward a woman with a large shopping bag.

He reached out his hand.

"This is it," I said. "He's about to steal again. And this time we're going to catch him!"

$ $ 6 $ $
Puzzles

The woman just handed the bag to the man!

"I don't think he's stealing the woman's shopping bag," Houdini said. "I think he's helping her carry it."

Houdini was right. The woman smiled and held on to the man's arm. She was probably his wife.

"Rats!" I said.

"Gerbils!" Houdini said.

He was teasing me. He doesn't like it when I say, "Rats!" He says it's not fair to blame innocent animals when something goes wrong.

"Let's keep looking," I said. "We'll find the thief."

"Maybe not," Houdini said. "Follow me."

Houdini led me through the mall. He kept telling me to hurry. But I was still looking at people's feet. I was still hoping to find a man wearing blue sneakers.

"Here we are," Houdini said.

We were standing by one of the exits.

It was the spot where the woman was robbed.

Houdini looked into the garbage can.

"Good," he said. "The bag with the vase is still here."

It was buried beneath some other trash—
a banana peel, a newspaper, two soda cans,
and a wrapper from an ice cream bar.

Houdini told me to take out the vase.

"Why?"

"Just take it out," he told me.

I thought, *Why don't you take it out?* But
I didn't say it.

I took the newspaper and used it to
move the garbage aside. I grabbed the red
bag from Sadie's Gift Shop. The pieces
from the broken vase were still in the bag.

I gave Houdini the bag. "Why do you
want the broken vase?" I asked.

"I'm going to put it back together," Houdini said. "It will be like a puzzle. I'm good
at puzzles."

Houdini thinks he's good at everything.

He fit the pieces together.

"It's not all there," I said. "You're missing a small piece from the side. And you're missing two more pieces from the bottom."

"Missing! That's just what I thought," Houdini said.

I started to look for the pieces on the floor.

"You can look for the missing pieces, but I don't think you'll find them," said

Houdini. "If this is where the vase broke, there should be lots of glass splinters. But I don't think you'll find any of those, either."

I looked on the floor. Houdini was right. There were no pieces of glass and no glass splinters.

"Maybe someone swept them up," I said.

Houdini pointed to the Sugar Stick candy bar wrapper. "That wouldn't still be here if someone swept up."

"What are you saying?"

Houdini smiled.

"The vase didn't break here. There is no thief in blue sneakers. That woman is trying to cheat the mall!"

7
Maybe I'm Wrong

"Houdini Foster," I said, "I have no idea what you're talking about."

Houdini spoke slowly, like he was explaining something to a small child. I hate it when he does that.

"The woman wasn't robbed at all," said Houdini slowly. "*She* broke the vase."

"Why would she want to do that?"

"She didn't *want* to break the vase. It was an accident."

Houdini put the pieces of the vase into the red shopping bag.

He said, "The woman bought a vase at Sadie's. Then maybe she dropped it. Or maybe her dog sat on it and broke it."

Now *he* was blaming an innocent animal! How did Houdini even know the woman had a dog?

Houdini went on.

"Vases at Sadic's are expensive. The woman must have read the article in the newspaper about the man whose shopping bag and wallet were stolen. The mall repaid him for everything in the shopping bag."

Houdini held up the red shopping bag. "So the woman brought the broken vase back here and pretended that a thief broke it. But there was no thief. That's why her description was so mixed up. The woman just *said* she was robbed so she could get her money back for the broken vase. But she didn't know the Great Houdini would be at the mall. She can't fool me!"

Houdini smiled.

He was so proud of himself.

"But what about the receipt?" I asked. "It had the time and the date on it. According to the receipt, she bought the vase right before the robbery. She didn't have time to take it home, break it, and bring it back."

Houdini looked at me.

His smile faded.

He didn't look so proud of himself anymore.

"Maybe I'm wrong," he said.

What!?!

That was the first time I had ever heard Houdini say that he might be wrong.

"Let's keep looking for blue sneakers," I said.

And that's what we did.

We found a small boy wearing blue sneakers. He was about four years old and holding on to his mother's hand. We didn't think he was the thief.

We kept walking and looking at people's feet.

"It's getting late," Houdini said after a while. "Let's just find my mom's gift and go to Dana's."

He didn't sound like the old "almost a genius" Houdini anymore. It must have been real hard for him to admit he was wrong.

We walked to Doug's. We were looking at the goldfish when Houdini grabbed my arm.

"Look," he whispered. "There she is."

The woman who was robbed was standing in the hand cream, mouthwash, and plastic bowl aisle.

The woman picked up a large jar of hand cream. Then she took it up to the cash register. She reached into her pocket, pulled out her wallet, and paid the man behind the register.

I whispered to Houdini, "I thought she said her wallet was stolen."

"I was right!" Houdini said. He was smiling again. "There was no thief. She *was* cheating the mall!"

Then Houdini stared at the woman. I
waved my hand in front of his eyes and he
didn't blink.

He was thinking.

"Of course," he mumbled. "There were two."

"Two wallets?"

"No," he said. "Why would anyone carry two wallets? Two vases."

Houdini turned toward the exit. He started to walk quickly out of Doug's.

"I'll get the guard," he called back to me. "You follow the woman. And don't let her get away!"

8
You Can't Go There!

The woman left the store. She went one way. Houdini went the other way.

"Wait!" I called to Houdini. "How will you find me?"

He didn't answer. He was already too far away.

The woman walked to a shoe store. I followed her. She looked in the store window. Then she went in.

I didn't go into the store. I was afraid she

would know I was following her. I sat on the bench just outside.

I watched and waited.

I sat there a long time. I saw people walk in the store to buy shoes and come out carrying what they bought.

But I didn't see the woman.

Suddenly I had a horrible thought.

Maybe there's a back door to the shoe store. Maybe she knew I was following her, and she went through the shoe store to lose me!

I hurried to the shoe store window. I looked in. There were a few people trying on shoes. There was a big pile of boxes. But I didn't see the woman.

I ran into the store. I had to find the back door. Maybe I could still catch her.

A man stuck out his foot just as I ran past. He was looking at a shoe. He almost tripped me!

I headed toward the door at the back of the store.

"Stop! You can't go there," one of the shoe store people told me.

He pointed to a sign.

EMPLOYEES ONLY

"I'm looking for the back way out of here," I said.

"Customers have to leave this store the same way they come in," the man said. "Through the front door."

I turned to walk out.

And then I saw her.

First I saw her foot. Then I saw her bright green dress. She was on the other side of a pile of boxes.

"I've shown you every shoe we have in your size," the shoe man said to her.

"Show me the blue one again," the woman told him. "The one with the nice little ribbon in front."

"Blue with a ribbon," the man mumbled. "Blue with a ribbon."

He took a box from the middle of the pile.

I walked to the other side of the store. I was hoping the woman wouldn't see me.

But she did. She reached for the blue shoes and looked right at me. She turned her head to the side a little. She wrinkled

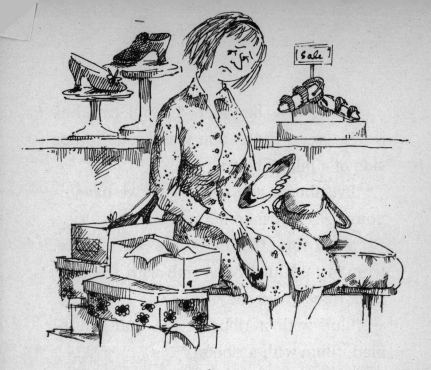

her eyes as if she was trying to remember something.

"Are you going to try these on or not?" the shoe man asked.

The woman shook her head. She put on her own shoes, stood up, and walked to the door.

Then she started to run.

9
Red 12

I ran after the woman. She ran out the mall exit to the parking lot.

She was getting away!

I was all alone. I was sure Houdini and the guard were looking for me in the mall. They would never find me out here.

There were thousands of cars in the parking lot. The woman ran down aisle Red 7. Then she ran across to aisle Red 8. She ran back to Red 7 and then to Red 6.

She forgot where she parked her car!

That happens to lots of people.

I remembered when it happened to my father. He used an emergency telephone in the parking lot and called the security guards. They drove him around until he found his car.

That's it! I thought.

There was a telephone at Red 10.

I picked it up.

A guard answered.

"I'm in Red 10," I said. I was talking fast. "I'm following a woman. She can't find her car. And she didn't buy shoes."

"What are you talking about?"

"The vase!" I said. "The vase. The thief didn't break it. There was no thief. The woman broke it!"

"Oh," the guard said. "I know who you are."

He knew all about the woman, Houdini, and the vase.

"Max and your friend are looking for you," he said. "Max is one of our guards. I'll call him on his portable telephone and tell him where to find you."

I thanked the guard and hung up. Then I looked for the woman in the green dress.

She was in Red 12.

She had found her car!

It was white with a big dent in one of the doors. The woman was opening the trunk when Max the guard tapped me on my shoulder and asked, "Where is she?"

I pointed.

Max hurried down Red 12. Houdini and I followed him.

When we got to the car, the trunk was open. There was a bag from Sadie's Gifts. Inside it was another vase.

Houdini was right. There *were* two vases.

Houdini is always right. That's because he's almost a genius.

The woman quickly shut the trunk.

"It's too late," the guard told her. "I know you tried to cheat the mall."

"I was the one who figured it out," said Houdini. "You bought two vases, didn't you?"

The woman turned and faced Houdini. She looked upset.

"Yes," the woman said softly.

"Why did you do it?" the guard asked.

"I bought the first vase last week. I brought it home and put the bag on my kitchen table. Then I put a bag of groceries right on top. The vase broke."

The woman looked at Max.

"I tried to glue it together. But I couldn't. Then I read about the robbery at the mall last week and how you repaid the man for what was stolen. That's when I decided to pretend that a thief broke my vase. I came back to the mall and bought another one just like it so I would have a receipt with the right date and time."

Houdini said, "What you did is just like what I do in my Magic Money Trick."

The woman looked at Houdini. Then she went on.

"I put the new vase in my car. Then I dropped the broken pieces from the first vase on the floor of the mall and yelled that I was robbed."

The woman took out her wallet. She took out the check for the broken vase.

"I can't keep this," she said. She handed the check to Max.

"I won't ever do anything like this again," the woman said.

Max told the woman she could go.

"I'm sorry," she said to Houdini and me. Then she got into her car and drove off.

"Good work!" Max told us. "You two deserve a reward for helping us prevent a crime. Come to my office."

We followed Max to his office.

The reward was a gift certificate. We could use it at any store in the mall.

Max asked us what name we wanted him to type on the certificate.

"I still don't have a gift for my mother," Houdini said. "Could we give it to her?"

"Sure," I said. Aunt Helen is so nice.

"Helen Foster," Houdini told Max.

Max typed in her name. He put the certificate in a fancy envelope and gave it to Houdini.

"Thanks," Houdini said. "Now I have something to give Mom on Mother's Day."

"Don't forget," I said. "It's from both of us."

We left the mall and started toward Dana's house.

Houdini looked at his watch.

I looked at my watch, too. It was five minutes past three.

"I told you we would be late for the meeting," Houdini said. "And I was right."

Of course he was right. Houdini is always right.

I hate that!

$ 10 $
The Great Houdini

Dana was on her front porch. She was waiting for us.

"You're late," she said. "You're always late."

"I'm worth waiting for," Houdini told her as he walked past. "I have a great trick to show you."

Dana and I followed him to the basement. Jordan, Melissa, Rachel, Daniel, Maria, and Tony were there.

Houdini went into the laundry room to prepare the trick. I found the card and the ashtray I had made for my mom. Dana had put them on top of the television.

Dana gave me some wrapping paper and some tape so I could wrap the ashtray.

Then Houdini came out of the laundry room. He was wearing his black cape and top hat.

He swirled his cape and said, "Get ready for the greatest magic trick ever. Get ready for Magic Money!"

Houdini waved a phony dollar bill in front of us.

"Daniel, please tear this money in half," he said.

Daniel took the Magic Money from Houdini.

"You know," Daniel said, "this isn't real money. If you try to spend it, you could get arrested."

"Just tear it in half," Houdini said.

Daniel tore the Magic Money in half.
Houdini put the torn money in an envelope. He sealed the envelope. He waved his
magic wand over the envelope and said,

"*Ala-kazam*, I am great. Yes, I am."

Then Houdini tore off the end of the envelope. He shook out the Magic Money. It was whole again.

"I AM GREAT! YES, I AM!" Houdini shouted.

"How did you do that?" Dana asked.

"Will you teach us the trick?" Tony asked.

Just then I remembered what Houdini said in the parking lot about how the two vases reminded him of his trick. Suddenly I knew why the money was whole again. I knew how the trick worked!

Houdini swirled his cape. Then he asked, "Who is the greatest magician since Harry Houdini?"

"YOU ARE!" the others shouted.

But I didn't shout. I started to wrap my Mother's Day gift.

I'm not almost a genius.

I'm not always right.

But I'm a good daughter.

The Magic Money Trick

by Bob Friedhoffer

EFFECT:

A torn dollar bill magically becomes whole again.

PROPS:

>A bottle of white glue
>
>A business-size envelope
>
>A green marker
>
>Scissors
>
>A sheet of white paper

PREPARATION:

- Using the green marker and the white paper, make two play one-dollar bills.
- Open the envelope. Place a line of

glue inside the envelope, halfway across. The line of glue should run up and down, from the bottom of the envelope straight up to the crease where the flap folds down. Press the front and back of the envelope together and allow the glue to dry.

• The envelope should now be divided into two sections, a left-hand section and a right-hand section. Take one of the play dollar bills and fold it in half. Place the folded bill into the left-hand section of the envelope.

• NOTE: If the dollar bill shows through the envelope, color or decorate the envelope with markers, crayons, or construction paper.

• Put the other dollar bill in your pocket.

ROUTINE AND PATTER:

- Take the play dollar bill out of your pocket and wave it in front of the audience. *"Ladies and gentlemen, I hold in my hand a special one-dollar bill. If this bill is torn in half, it will magically put itself back together."*

- Call up a volunteer from the audience. Ask the volunteer to rip the bill in half.

"I will now put the two halves of the Magic Money into the envelope."

- Pick up the envelope and show it to the audience.

- Place the torn bill into the empty *right-hand* section of the envelope. Seal the envelope. Then say some magic words, such as "abracadabra."

- Rip open the envelope along the *left-hand* edge. Be careful not to rip the folded dollar bill you placed inside earlier.

- Turn the envelope sideways and shake it so the folded dollar bill falls out. *"Observe! Just as I promised, the dollar bill has magically put itself back together."*

- Open the folded dollar bill and hold it out for the audience to see. The audience will be amazed that the dollar bill is whole again!

Onion Sundaes

"My cousin says she doesn't like onions," Houdini said. "I guess I'll have to change this onion into something she does like."

Houdini dropped the onion into the top of the red paper tube.

He waved his magic wand and said, "*Ala-kazam,* I am great. Yes, I am."

Then he picked up the tube.

There on the table was a jar of chocolate syrup!

"How did you do that?" I asked.

From *Onion Sundaes*
(A Houdini Club Magic Mystery book)
by David A. Adler

How do you make a playing card disappear?
Find out in...
Wacky Jacks

"Now put the Wacky Jack back on the deck," said Houdini.

Mr. Fish put the card on top of the deck.

Houdini took out his magic wand. He waved it over the cards. "*Ala-kazam,* I am great. Yes, I am," he said.

Houdini tapped the deck with the wand and gave it to Mr. Fish. "Now see if you can find the Wacky Jack."

Mr. Fish turned the cards over.

The Wacky Jack was gone.

From *Wacky Jacks*
(A Houdini Club Magic Mystery book)
by David A. Adler

How do you predict what someone will pick?
Find out in...
Lucky Stars

I pointed to the red star.

"Janet, please turn over the red star," Houdini said.

I turned over the red star. There was a message written there. I read it aloud: "You will pick the red star."

"Wait a minute," I said. "That's not so amazing. I bet there's a message on the backs of the blue and yellow stars, too."

"Why don't you check?" he said.

I turned over the blue star. Then I turned over the yellow star.

The backs of those stars were blank.

From *Lucky Stars*
(A Houdini Club Magic Mystery book)
by David A. Adler

About the Authors

DAVID A. ADLER was one of six children in his family. "I used to do magic tricks to get attention," he says. "Now I write books to get attention!"

David has written many books for kids, including the acclaimed Cam Jansen mysteries and the Picture Book Biography series. He lives in New York with his wife and their three sons.

BOB FRIEDHOFFER, known as the "Madman of Magic," created the Magic Money Trick. He has been a magician for over fifteen years and has even performed at the White House.

Bob has written over twenty-five books for children and young adults. He currently lives and works in New York City.